THE AWARD BOOK OF
TALES & RHYMES

Illustrated by Ray Mutimer

AWARD PUBLICATIONS LIMITED

Contents

Rhymes

Stories

This Little Pig

This little pig went to market,

This little pig stayed at home,

This little pig had roast beef,

This little pig had none,

And this little pig cried,
Wee-wee-wee-wee-wee,
I can't find my way home.

8

Twinkle, Twinkle, Little Star

Twinkle, twinkle, little star,
How I wonder what you are!
Up above the world so high,
Like a diamond in the sky.

When the blazing sun is gone,
When he nothing shines upon,
Then you show your little light,
Twinkle, twinkle, all the night.

As your bright and tiny spark,
Lights the traveller in the dark,
Though I know not what you are,
Twinkle, twinkle, little star.

Mary Had a Little Lamb

Mary had a little lamb,
Its fleece was white as snow;
And everywhere that Mary went
The lamb was sure to go.

It followed her to school one day,
Which was against the rule;
It made the children laugh and play
To see a lamb at school.

And so the teacher turned it out,
But still it lingered near,
And waited patiently about
Till Mary did appear.

Why does the lamb love Mary so?
The eager children cry;
Why, Mary loves the lamb, you know,
The teacher did reply.

Humpty Dumpty

Humpty Dumpty sat on a wall,
Humpty Dumpty had a great fall;
All the king's horses
    and all the king's men,
Couldn't put Humpty together again.

Old Mother Hubbard

Old Mother Hubbard
Went to the cupboard,
To fetch her poor dog a bone;
But when she came there
The cupboard was bare
And so the poor dog had none.

Little Boy Blue

Little Boy Blue,
Come blow your horn,
The sheep's in the meadow,
The cow's in the corn.

But where is the boy
Who looks after the sheep?
He's under a haycock,
Fast asleep.

Will you wake him?
No, not I,
For if I do,
He's sure to cry.

Little Robin Redbreast

Little Robin Redbreast
Sat upon a rail;
Niddle-noddle went his head,
Wiggle-waggle went his tail.

Pussy Cat, Pussy Cat

Pussy cat, pussy cat, where have you been?
I've been to London to look at the queen.
Pussy cat, pussy cat, what did you there?
I frightened a little mouse under her chair.

Hickory, Dickory, Dock

Hickory, dickory, dock,
The mouse ran up the clock.
The clock struck one,
The mouse ran down,
Hickory, dickory, dock.

Incey Wincey Spider

Incey Wincey spider
Climbing up the spout;
Down came the rain
And washed the spider out;
Out came the sunshine
And dried up all the rain;
Incey Wincey spider
Climbing up again.

Little Jack Horner

Little Jack Horner
Sat in the corner,
Eating a Christmas pie;
He put in his thumb,
And pulled out a plum,
And said, What a good boy am I!

Polly Put the Kettle On

Polly put the kettle on,
Polly put the kettle on,
Polly put the kettle on,
We'll all have tea.

Sukey take it off again,
Sukey take it off again,
Sukey take it off again,
They've all gone away.

Boys and Girls Come Out to Play

Boys and girls come out to play,
The moon doth shine as bright as day.
Leave your supper and leave your sleep,
And join your playfellows in the street.
Come with a whoop and come with a call,
Come with a good will or not at all.
Up the ladder and down the wall,
A half-penny loaf will serve us all;
You find milk and I'll find flour,
And we'll have a pudding in half an hour.

16

Mary, Mary, Quite Contrary

Mary, Mary, quite contrary,
How does your garden grow?
With silver bells and cockle shells,
And pretty maids all in a row.

Georgie Porgie

Georgie Porgie, pudding and pie,
Kissed the girls and made them cry;
When the boys came out to play,
Georgie Porgie ran away.

Tom, Tom, the Piper's Son

Tom, Tom, the piper's son,
Stole a pig and away he run;
The pig was eat
And Tom was beat,
And Tom went howling down the street.

Little Tommy Tucker

Little Tommy Tucker,
Sings for his supper:
What shall we give him?
White bread and butter.
How shall we cut it
Without a knife?
How will he be married
Without a wife?

18

Baa, Baa, Black Sheep

Baa, baa, black sheep,
Have you any wool?
Yes, sir, yes, sir,
Three bags full;
One for the master,
And one for
   the dame,
And one for
   the little boy
Who lives down the lane.

Rub-a-dub-dub

Rub-a-dub-dub,
Three men in a tub,
And how do you think they got there?
The butcher, the baker,
The candlestick-maker,
They all jumped out of a rotten potato,
'Twas enough to make a man stare.

19

One, Two, Buckle My Shoe

One, two,
Buckle my shoe;

Three, four,
Knock at the door;

Five, six,
Pick up sticks;

Seven, eight,
Lay them straight;

Nine, ten,
A big fat hen;

20

Eleven, twelve,
Dig and delve;

Thirteen, fourteen,
Maids a-courting;

Fifteen, sixteen,
Maids in the kitchen;

Seventeen, eighteen,
Maids in waiting;

Nineteen, twenty,
My plate's empty.

Hey Diddle Diddle

Hey diddle diddle,
The cat and the fiddle,
The cow jumped over the moon;
The little dog laughed
To see such sport,
And the dish ran away with the spoon.

Goosey, Goosey Gander

Goosey, goosey gander,
Whither shall I wander?
Upstairs and downstairs
And in my lady's chamber.
There I met an old man
Who would not say his prayers.
I took him by the left leg
And threw him down the stairs.

Ring-a-ring o' Roses

Ring-a-ring o' roses,
A pocket full of posies,
A-tishoo! A-tishoo!
We all fall down.

There Was an Old Woman Who Lived in a Shoe

There was an old woman who lived in a shoe,
She had so many children she didn't know what to do;
She gave them some broth without any bread;
She whipped them all soundly and put them to bed.

23

The Wheels on the Bus

The wheels on the bus go round and round,
Round and round, round and round;
The wheels on the bus go round and round,
All over town.

The doors on the bus go open and shut,
Open and shut, open and shut;
The doors on the bus go open and shut,
All over town.

The people on the bus step out and in,
Out and in, out and in;
The people on the bus step out and in,
All over town.

The windows on the bus slide up and down,
Up and down, up and down;
The windows on the bus slide up and down,
All over town.

The wipers on the bus go swish, swish, swish,
Swish, swish, swish; swish, swish, swish;
The wipers on the bus go swish, swish, swish,
All over town.

The riders on the bus go bumpity-bump,
Bumpity-bump, bumpity-bump;
The riders on the bus go bumpity-bump,
All over town.

The babies on the bus cry Wah! wah! wah!
Wah! wah! wah! Wah! wah! wah!
The babies on the bus cry Wah! wah! wah!
All over town.

The mothers on the bus go Shh! shh! shh!
Shh! shh! shh! Shh! shh! shh!
The mothers on the bus go Shh! shh! shh!
All over town.

The wheels on the bus go round and round,
Round and round, round and round;
The wheels on the bus go round and round,
All over town.

Little Bo-peep

Little Bo-peep has lost her sheep,
And can't tell where to find them;
Leave them alone, and they'll come home,
Bringing their tails behind them.

Little Bo-peep fell fast asleep,
And dreamt she heard them bleating;
But when she awoke, she found it a joke,
For they were still all fleeting.

Then up she took her little crook,
Determined for to find them;
She found them indeed,
    but it made her heart bleed,
For they'd left their tails behind them.

Hush-a-bye, Baby

Hush-a-bye, baby, on the tree top,
When the wind blows the cradle will rock;
When the bough breaks the cradle will fall,
Down will come baby, cradle, and all.

Little Miss Muffet

Little Miss Muffet
Sat on a tuffet,
Eating her curds and whey;
There came a big spider,
Who sat down beside her
And frightened Miss Muffet away.

Little Tommy Tittlemouse

Little Tommy Tittlemouse
Lived in a little house;
He caught fishes
In other men's ditches.

Sing a Song of Sixpence

Sing a song of sixpence,
A pocket full of rye;
Four and twenty blackbirds
Baked in a pie.

When the pie was opened,
The birds began to sing;
Was not that a dainty dish,
To set before the king?

The king was in his counting-house,
Counting out his money;
The queen was in the parlour,
Eating bread and honey.

The maid was in the garden,
Hanging out the clothes,
When down came a blackbird,
And pecked off her nose.

The North Wind Doth Blow

The north wind doth blow,
And we shall have snow,
And what will poor robin do then?
        Poor thing.
He'll sit in a barn,
And keep himself warm,
And hide his head under his wing.
        Poor thing.

Lucy Locket
Lucy Locket lost her pocket,
Kitty Fisher found it;
Not a penny was there in it,
Only ribbon round it.

Old King Cole

Old King Cole was a merry old soul,
And a merry old soul was he;
He called for his pipe
    and he called for his bowl,
And he called for his fiddlers three.

Every fiddler, he had a fiddle,
And a very fine fiddle had he;
Twee tweedle dee, tweedle dee,
    went the fiddlers.
Oh, there's none so rare as can compare
With Old King Cole and his fiddlers three.

There Was an Old Woman

There was an old woman tossed up in a basket,
Seventeen times as high as the moon;
Where she was going I couldn't but ask it,
For in her hand she carried a broom.
Old woman, old woman, old woman, quoth I,
Where are you going to up so high?
To brush the cobwebs off the sky!
May I go with you?
Aye, by-and-by.

Oranges and Lemons

Oranges and lemons,
Say the bells of St Clement's.

You owe me five farthings,
Say the bells of St Martin's.

When will you pay me?
Say the bells of Old Bailey.

When I grow rich,
Say the bells of Shoreditch.

When will that be?
Say the bells of Stepney.

I'm sure I don't know,
Says the great bell at Bow.

Here comes a candle to light you to bed,
Here comes a chopper to chop off your head.

31

London Bridge

London Bridge is falling down,
Falling down, falling down,
London Bridge is falling down,
My fair lady.

Build it up with wood and clay,
Wood and clay, wood and clay,
Build it up with wood and clay,
My fair lady.

Wood and clay will wash away,
Wash away, wash away,
Wood and clay will wash away,
My fair lady.

Build it up with iron and steel,
Iron and steel, iron and steel,
Build it up with iron and steel,
My fair lady.

I Had a Little Nut Tree

I had a little nut tree,
Nothing would it bear
But a silver nutmeg
And a golden pear;
The King of Spain's daughter
Came to visit me,
And all for the sake
Of my little nut tree.

Iron and steel will bend and bow,
Bend and bow, bend and bow,
Iron and steel will bend and bow,
My fair lady.

Build it up with silver and gold,
Silver and gold, silver and gold,
Build it up with silver and gold,
My fair lady.

Silver and gold will be stolen away,
Stolen away, stolen away,
Silver and gold will be stolen away,
My fair lady.

Set a man to watch all night,
Watch all night, watch all night,
Set a man to watch all night,
My fair lady.

Rain, Rain, Go Away

Rain, rain, go away,
Come again another day.

If I Had a Donkey

If I had a donkey that wouldn't go,
Would I beat him? Oh, no, no.
I'd put him in the barn and give him some corn,
The best little donkey that ever was born.

Daffy-down-dilly

Daffy-down-dilly is new come to town.
With a yellow petticoat, and a green gown.

The Little Black Dog

The little black dog ran round the house,
And set the bull a-roaring,
And drove the monkey in the boat,
Who set the oars a-rowing,
And scared the cock upon the rock,
Who cracked his throat with crowing.

To Market, to Market

To market, to market, to buy a fat pig,
Home again, home again, jiggety-jig;
To market, to market, to buy a fat hog,
Home again, home again, jiggety-jog.

The Owl and the Pussy-cat

The Owl and the Pussy-cat went to sea
In a beautiful pea-green boat,
They took some honey, and plenty of money,
Wrapped up in a five-pound note.
The Owl looked up to the stars above,
And sang to a small guitar,
"O lovely Pussy! O Pussy, my love,
What a beautiful Pussy you are,
    You are,
    You are!
What a beautiful Pussy you are!"

Pussy said to the Owl, "You elegant fowl!
How charmingly sweet you sing!
O let us be married! too long have we tarried:
But what shall we do for a ring?"
They sailed away, for a year and a day,
To the land where the Bong-tree grows
And there in a wood a Piggy-wig stood
With a ring at the end of his nose,
    His nose,
    His nose,
With a ring at the end of his nose.

"Dear Pig, are you willing to sell for one shilling
Your ring?" Said the Piggy, "I will."
So they took it away, and were married next day
By the Turkey who lives on the hill.
They dined on mince, and slices of quince,
Which they ate with a runcible spoon;
And hand in hand, on the edge of the sand,
They danced by the light of the moon,
    The moon,
    The moon,
They danced by the light of the moon.

The Walrus and the Carpenter

The sun was shining on the sea,
Shining with all his might:
He did his very best to make
The billows smooth and bright –
And this was odd, because it was
The middle of the night.

The moon was shining sulkily,
Because she thought the sun
Had got no business to be there
After the day was done –
"It's very rude of him," she said,
"To come and spoil the fun!"

The sea was wet as wet could be,
The sands were dry as dry.
You could not see a cloud, because
No cloud was in the sky:
No birds were flying overhead –
There were no birds to fly.

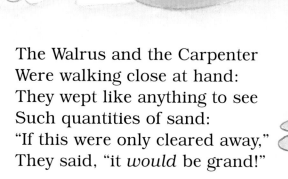

The Walrus and the Carpenter
Were walking close at hand:
They wept like anything to see
Such quantities of sand:
"If this were only cleared away,"
They said, "it *would* be grand!"

"If seven maids with seven mops
Swept it for half a year,
Do you suppose," the Walrus said,
"That they could get it clear?"
"I doubt it," said the Carpenter,
And shed a bitter tear.

"O Oysters, come and walk with us!"
The Walrus did beseech.
"A pleasant walk, a pleasant talk,
Along the briny beach:
We cannot do with more than four,
To give a hand to each."

The eldest Oyster looked at him,
But never a word he said:
The eldest Oyster winked his eye,
And shook his heavy head –
Meaning to say he did not choose
To leave his oyster-bed.

But four young Oysters hurried up,
All eager to the treat:
Their coats were brushed, their faces washed,
Their shoes were clean and neat –
And this was odd, because, you know,
They hadn't any feet.

Four other Oysters followed them,
And yet another four;
And thick and fast they came at last,
And more, and more, and more –
All hopping through the frothy waves,
And scrambling to the shore.

The Walrus and the Carpenter
Walked on a mile or so,
And then they rested on a rock
Conveniently low:
And all the little Oysters stood
And waited in a row.

"The time has come," the Walrus said,
"To talk of many things:
Of shoes – and ships – and sealing wax –
Of cabbages – and – kings –
And why the sea is boiling hot –
And whether pigs have wings."

"But wait a bit," the Oysters cried,
"Before we have our chat;
For some of us are out of breath,
And all of us are fat!"
"No hurry!" said the Carpenter.
They thanked him much for that.

"A loaf of bread," the Walrus said,
"Is what we chiefly need:
Pepper and vinegar besides
Are very good indeed –
Now, if you're ready, Oysters dear,
We can begin to feed."

"But not on us!" the Oysters cried,
Turning a little blue.
"After such kindness, that would be,
A dismal thing to do!"
"The night is fine," the Walrus said.
"Do you admire the view?

"It was so kind of you to come!
And you are very nice!"
The Carpenter said nothing but
"Cut us another slice.
I wish you were not quite so deaf –
I've had to ask you twice!"

"It seems a shame," the Walrus said,
"To play them such a trick.
After we've brought them out so far,
And made them trot so quick!"
The Carpenter said nothing but
"The butter's spread too thick!"

"I weep for you," the Walrus said:
"I deeply sympathise."
With sobs and tears he sorted out
Those of the largest size,
Holding his pocket-handkerchief
Before his streaming eyes.

"O Oysters," said the Carpenter,
"You've had a pleasant run!
Shall we be trotting home again?"
But answer came there none –
And this was scarcely odd, because
They'd eaten every one.

Old Mother Goose

Old Mother Goose, when
She wanted to wander,
Would ride through the air
On a very fine gander.

Mother Goose had a house,
'Twas built in a wood,
Where an owl at the door
For a sentinel stood.

41

Who Has Seen the Wind?

Who has seen the wind?
Neither I nor you:
But when the leaves hang trembling,
The wind is passing through.
Who has seen the wind?
Neither you nor I:
But when the trees bow down their heads,
The wind is passing by.

Ride a Cock-horse

Ride a cock-horse to Banbury Cross,
To see a fine lady upon a white horse;
Rings on her fingers and bells on her toes,
And she shall have music wherever she goes.

Diddlety, Diddlety, Dumpty

Diddlety, diddlety, dumpty,
The cat ran up the plum-tree;
Half a crown
To fetch her down,
Diddlety, diddlety, dumpty.

A Wise Old Owl Lived in an Oak

A wise old owl lived in an oak;
The more he saw the less he spoke;
The less he spoke the more he heard.
Why can't we all be like that wise old bird?

Hark, Hark, the Dogs Do Bark

Hark, hark,
The dogs do bark,
The beggars are coming to town;
Some in rags,
And some in jags,
And one in a velvet gown.

Thirty Days Hath September

Thirty days hath September,
April, June and November;
All the rest have thirty-one,
Excepting February alone,
And that has twenty-eight days clear
And twenty-nine in each leap year.

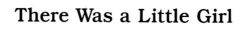

There Was a Little Girl

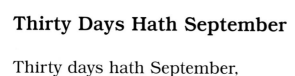

There was a little girl, and she had a little curl
Right in the middle of her forehead;
When she was good, she was very, very good
But when she was bad, she was horrid.

Simple Simon

Simple Simon met a pieman,
Going to the fair;
Says Simple Simon to the pieman,
Let me taste your ware.

Says the pieman to Simple Simon,
Show me first your penny;
Says Simple Simon to the pieman,
Indeed I have not any.

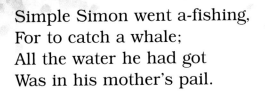

Simple Simon went a-fishing,
For to catch a whale;
All the water he had got
Was in his mother's pail.

Simple Simon went to look
If plums grew on a thistle;
He pricked his finger very much,
Which made poor Simon whistle.

Solomon Grundy

Solomon Grundy,
Born on a Monday,
Christened on Tuesday,
Married on Wednesday,
Took ill on Thursday,
Worse on Friday,
Died on Saturday,
Buried on Sunday.
This is the end
Of Solomon Grundy.

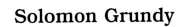

You are Old Father William

"You are old Father William," the young man said,
"And your hair has become very white;
And yet you incessantly stand on your head –
Do you think, at your age, it is right?"

"In my youth," Father William replied to his son,
"I feared it might injure the brain;
But now that I'm perfectly sure I have none,
Why, I do it again and again."

"You are old," said the youth, "as I mentioned before,
And have grown most uncommonly fat;
Yet you turned a back-somersault in at the door –
Pray what is the reason of that?"

"In my youth," said the sage, as he shook his grey locks,
"I kept all my limbs very supple
By the use of this ointment – one shilling the box –
Allow me to sell you a couple?"

"You are old," said the youth, "and your jaws are too weak
For anything tougher than suet;
Yet you finished the goose, with the bones and the beak –
Pray, how did you manage to do it?"

"In my youth," said his father, "I took to the law,
And argued each case with my wife;
And the muscular strength which it gave to my jaw,
Has lasted the rest of my life."

"You are old," said the youth, "one would hardly suppose
That your eye was as steady as ever;
Yet you balanced an eel on the end of your nose –
What made you so awfully clever?"

"I have answered three questions, and that is enough,"
Said his father. "Don't give yourself airs!
Do you think I can listen all day to such stuff?
Be off, or I'll kick you downstairs!"

Yankee Doodle Came to Town

Yankee Doodle came to town,
Riding on a pony;
He stuck a feather in his cap,
And called it macaroni.

The House that Jack Built

This is the house that Jack built.

This is the malt
That lay in the house that Jack built.

This is the rat,
That ate the malt
That lay in the house that Jack built.

This is the cat,
That killed the rat,
That ate the malt
That lay in the house that Jack built.

This is the dog that worried the cat,
That killed the rat,
That ate the malt
That lay in the house that Jack built.

This is the cow with the crumpled horn,
That tossed the dog,
That worried the cat,
That killed the rat,
That ate the malt
That lay in the house that Jack built.

This is the maiden all forlorn,
That milked the cow with the crumpled horn,
That tossed the dog,
That worried the cat,
That killed the rat,
That ate the malt
That lay in the house that Jack built.

This is the man all tattered and torn,
That kissed the maiden all forlorn,
That milked the cow with the crumpled horn,
That tossed the dog,
That worried the cat,
That killed the rat,
That ate the malt
That lay in the house that Jack built.

This is the priest all shaven and shorn,
That married the man all tattered and torn,
That kissed the maiden all forlorn,
That milked the cow with the crumpled horn,
That tossed the dog,
That worried the cat,
That killed the rat,
That ate the malt
That lay in the house that Jack built.

This is the cock that crowed in the morn,
That waked the priest all shaven and shorn,
That married the man all tattered and torn,
That kissed the maiden all forlorn,
That milked the cow with the crumpled horn,
That tossed the dog,
That worried the cat,
That killed the rat,
That ate the malt
That lay in the house that Jack built.

I Saw a Ship a-Sailing

I saw a ship a-sailing,
A-sailing on the sea,
And oh, but it was laden
With pretty things for thee!

There were comfits in the cabin,
And apples in the hold;
The sails were made of silk,
And the masts were all of gold.

The four-and-twenty sailors,
That stood between the decks,
Were four-and-twenty white mice
With chains about their necks.

The captain was a duck
With a packet on his back,
And when the ship began to move
The captain said, Quack! Quack!

The Elves and the Shoemaker

There was once a very poor shoemaker who lived with his wife above their shop. They were so poor that they had little money to buy food and the shoemaker had only enough leather to make one more pair of shoes.

That evening the shoemaker cut the leather very carefully into pieces. He laid them out on the top of his workbench so that they would be ready for him to sew into a pair of shoes the next day. Then he went upstairs to join his wife.

In the morning the shoemaker opened up his shop and then went into the workshop to start the sad task of sewing together the pieces of leather for his last pair of shoes. But when he looked at his workbench he was astonished. In place of the pieces of leather there was the most beautiful pair of shoes.

He picked them up carefully and saw that the small stitches were all the same length. The leather had been polished so highly that he could see his face in the wonderful finish. Who could have made them? He ran to the bottom of the stairs and called to his wife, "My dear, come down and see what I've found." His wife couldn't believe it when she saw the perfectly made pair of shoes.

The shoemaker put them in the window of the shop. Later that morning a rich woman passing by saw the shoes in the window. Immediately she came into the shop and tried the shoes on. They fitted perfectly.

"How much are they?" she asked.

"Two crowns," said the shoemaker.

The rich woman placed five crowns in the shoemaker's hand and left, absolutely delighted. The shoemaker, too, was pleased because he now had the money to buy enough leather to make two pairs of shoes, and there would be sufficient money left over to buy some food.

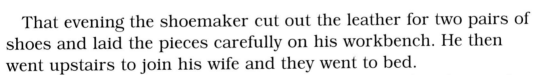

That evening the shoemaker cut out the leather for two pairs of shoes and laid the pieces carefully on his workbench. He then went upstairs to join his wife and they went to bed.

In the morning the shoemaker again opened up his shop and went into the workshop. He was amazed. In place of the pieces of leather he had left on the workbench were two pairs of shoes. He picked up the shoes and admired how beautifully they had been made. And the finish was wonderful; they had been polished until they shone.

He put the two pairs of shoes in his shop window. Later that day a rich man was passing the shop, and when he saw the shoes he came in to ask if he could try them on. They fitted perfectly. The rich man was so pleased with the shoes that the shoemaker again received more money than he asked for. The shoemaker was then able to buy the leather to make four pairs of shoes.

Next day, when he opened up the shop and went into the workshop, he found four pairs of shoes. He sold these very quickly.

And so it went on day after day. Each night the shoemaker cut out the pieces of leather and in the morning there were finished shoes, made with delicate, small and even stitches, each shining beautifully. The shoemaker's fame spread far and wide and he, too, became rich.

Christmas was approaching and one morning, as the shoemaker took the finished shoes from his workbench to the shop window, he said to his wife, "We should try to find out who is sewing these beautiful shoes for us."

"Why don't we leave the leather pieces on the workbench and then hide behind the door to see who makes the shoes in the night?" his wife suggested.

That evening after supper the shoemaker cut up the leather into pieces and he and his wife then hid behind the door of the workshop. They waited and waited and eventually the shop door opened and in rushed two little elves. They had bare feet and very ragged clothes and each carried a little bag over his shoulder.

Very quickly they took their tools out of the bags and they were soon stitching and hammering away. The leather pieces were changed as if by magic into beautiful shoes which they polished until they shone. Just as quickly the elves packed up their bags and went out through the shop doorway.

As they climbed into bed the shoemaker said to his wife, "We must repay the elves for their great kindness. We are very well off now and it is all due to the elves."

In the morning the shoemaker's wife said to her husband, "I am going to make the elves some new clothes to replace the ragged ones they were wearing."

The shoemaker scratched his head and said, "And I shall make them some tiny boots for their bare feet."

So that day they worked away making new outfits for the elves. In the evening the shoemaker and his wife wrapped the clothes up in pretty paper and left them on the workbench. "Now let's hide like we did last night," he said to his wife, and they waited to see if the elves came back again.

During the middle of the night the elves came rushing in through the shop door but instead of leather pieces they found the tiny parcels. When they opened the presents they were delighted. They sang as they pulled on each item. And in their tiny leather boots they danced on the workbench, singing:

"The shoemaker is no longer poor,
We needn't help him any more,
So we can run out through the door."

And that's exactly what they did; they sped off into the night and that was the last time that the shoemaker and his wife saw the little elves.

But the shoemaker and his wife were very happy. They were famous and they were never poor again!

The Gingerbread Man

Once upon a time a little old man and a little old woman lived in a little old house. Every week the little old woman baked cakes and puddings and lots of other nice things to eat.

"I am going to bake something different this week," she said to her husband. "I'll bake a gingerbread man." She reached up into the cupboard for the ingredients and put them on the kitchen table.

The old woman quickly mixed everything together and made a gingerbread man. She gave him eyes made from currants, a nose made from pastry, and finally she cut out a mouth, giving him a great big smile. She popped him in the oven to bake, but after a few minutes she heard a voice crying, "Let me out! Let me out!"

The little old woman opened the door of the oven and the gingerbread man leaped up off the baking tray, down on to the kitchen floor, and ran away. He dashed out of the kitchen door into the garden and ran off as fast as he could.

"Come back, come back," called the little old man and the little old woman. But the gingerbread man just kept running. He called back over his shoulder:

"Run, run, as fast as you can,
You can't catch me,
I'm the gingerbread man!"

After a while he came to a field, so he climbed over a stile and ran on. A cow chewing grass in the middle of the field mooed, "Hey, little man! Stop! You look good enough to eat."

But the gingerbread man just ran faster, and although the cow ran and ran she couldn't catch him. He just looked over his shoulder and shouted:

"Run, run, as fast as you can,
You can't catch me,
I'm the gingerbread man!"

A little while later, in the next field, the gingerbread man met a horse. The horse looked at the gingerbread man running through the field and said, "Stop, little man, you look good enough to eat."

But the gingerbread man just laughed and turned round as he ran, shouting over his shoulder:

"Run, run, as fast as you can,
You can't catch me,
I'm the gingerbread man!"

The horse ran and ran after the gingerbread man but he couldn't catch him.

"I've run away from a little old man, a little old woman and a cow and I've no intention of being caught now," shouted the little man. On and on he ran, getting faster and faster.

As he went past a hedge he saw a fox. "Stop! Stop!" said the fox. "Let's talk." But the gingerbread man was very wary of the fox and he ran away as fast as he could. Looking over his shoulder he shouted:

"Run, run, as fast as you can,
You can't catch me,
I'm the gingerbread man!"

He crossed another field but then his way was blocked by a river. "What am I going to do now?" he thought. The fox was fast enough to catch up with the gingerbread man and he offered to help him.

"Do you wish to cross the river?" asked the fox.

"Yes I do," replied the gingerbread man.

"Very well then, jump up on to my tail and hold on tightly while I swim across," said the fox. "You will stay safe and dry."

The gingerbread man grabbed the fox's tail and the fox started to swim across. But as he reached deeper water the fox said, "You are very heavy; crawl on to my back and I'll be able to support you better."

The gingerbread man did as the fox suggested but a little further on the fox's back started to get wet. "Climb on to my head," said the fox. The gingerbread man wanted to stay dry so again he followed the fox's suggestion. As the fox started to sink even more below the water he said, "Climb on to my nose and you won't get wet." The gingerbread man moved on to the fox's nose.

But just as they reached the far bank of the river the crafty fox threw the gingerbread man high into the air. As he tumbled down the gingerbread man fell right into the fox's mouth. *Crunch* went the fox, and that was the end of the little gingerbread man.

So, fast as he was, the gingerbread man couldn't beat the cunning fox.

The Three Billy-goats Gruff

Once upon a time there were three billy-goat brothers called Gruff. They lived in a land full of high mountains and deep valleys, where the ground was very stony and very little grew. One day they decided to go in search of some tender green grass.

The goats had not travelled very far when they came to a river. On the far side of the river was a meadow where the green grass grew thick and lush. But to cross to the other side they would have to walk over a rickety wooden bridge. The two older brothers knew that under the bridge lived a fierce, bad tempered and very ugly troll. "How are we going to get across safely?" said the eldest billy-goat.

The sight of all that grass soon became too much for the youngest billy-goat and he decided to go across.

"Wait!" the older brothers bleated. "You'll be gobbled up by the troll." But the little billy-goat was already on the bridge. His little hooves went *trip-trap, trip-trap* as he walked over the wooden boards.

The noise woke up the troll who screamed out, "Who's that trip-trapping over my bridge?" and poked his head up over the side of the bridge. When the youngest billy-goat saw his horrible face he was very frightened.

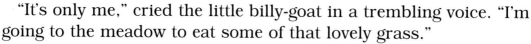

"It's only me," cried the little billy-goat in a trembling voice. "I'm going to the meadow to eat some of that lovely grass."

"Then I'm coming to gobble you up," said the troll, licking his lips with his huge tongue.

The smallest billy-goat Gruff summoned up all his courage and said, "You don't want to eat me. I'm only tiny. My brother is following shortly and he's much fatter than I am."

The troll dropped back under the bridge and the little billy-goat Gruff trip-trapped across the bridge and into the meadow. And there he began to feast on the lush green grass.

The older brothers now had to get across the bridge. Soon the middle-sized billy-goat Gruff reached the bridge and began to cross. *Trip-trap, trip-trap* went his hooves on the wooden planks. When he was halfway across the greedy troll popped his head up over the side of the bridge. "Who's that trip-trapping over my bridge?" he shouted gruffly.

"It's only me," bleated the middle-sized billy-goat Gruff. "I am off to the meadow to eat some of that lovely green grass."

"Then I'm coming to gobble you up," said the troll, licking his lips and showing his fierce-looking teeth.

The middle-sized billy-goat Gruff summoned up all his courage and said, "You don't want to eat me. My brother is following shortly, and he's much, much fatter than I am."

The troll dropped back under the bridge, licking his lips hungrily, and the middle-sized billy-goat Gruff trip-trapped across to the far side of the bridge and into the meadow. There he feasted on the lush green grass.

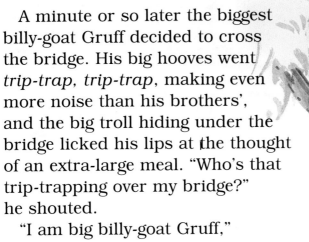

A minute or so later the biggest billy-goat Gruff decided to cross the bridge. His big hooves went *trip-trap, trip-trap*, making even more noise than his brothers', and the big troll hiding under the bridge licked his lips at the thought of an extra-large meal. "Who's that trip-trapping over my bridge?" he shouted.

"I am big billy-goat Gruff," said the biggest billy-goat in a gruff voice. "I am going across the bridge to reach the meadow so that I can eat the lovely green grass."

"Oh no, you're not!" the greedy troll shouted. "I'm coming to gobble you up." And with that the troll heaved himself up over the side of the bridge and stood face to face with the oldest billy-goat. But he wasn't expecting to see such a big billy-goat. With his huge horns and long legs, the biggest billy-goat Gruff looked enormous to the troll, who turned round to escape back under the bridge. As he did, the biggest billy-goat Gruff put his head down and charged. With one toss of his head the biggest billy-goat Gruff butted the troll high into the air, off the bridge and into the water with a huge splash. Then the biggest billy-goat Gruff trip-trapped his way rather proudly across the bridge and joined his brothers to eat the lush green grass.

The troll was carried away by the river, never to be seen again, and everyone was delighted because once more it was safe to cross the bridge. And the three billy-goats Gruff lived happily ever after in their green meadow.

Goldilocks and the Three Bears

Once upon a time there were three bears who lived in a pretty little house in the middle of a wood. There was Father Bear, a great big bear; Mother Bear, a medium-sized bear; and Baby Bear, a tiny little bear.

Their house was kept very clean and tidy. Nothing was out of place and their beds, chairs, knives, forks and spoons were each in three sizes, one for a big bear, one for a medium-sized bear and one for a tiny bear.

One morning Mother Bear made some porridge for breakfast. She spooned out three different sized portions for the three bears. One portion she put in a tiny bowl, another in a medium-sized bowl and the last in a great big bowl. But when they sat down at the table the porridge was far too hot to eat. Father Bear said, "While we are waiting for it to cool, let us go for a walk through the woods."

On the edge of the wood lived a naughty little girl with long golden hair. She was called Goldilocks. As she was passing the bears' house on her way to the village shop nearby she noticed that the front door had been left open. She just had to look inside. She peeped round the edge of the door and saw no sign of the bears.

But on the table she saw three steaming bowls of porridge.

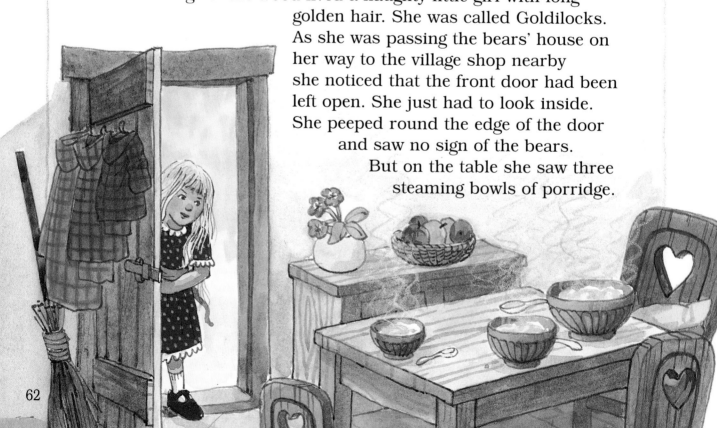

Goldilocks couldn't resist trying some of the porridge because she hadn't eaten any breakfast and she was hungry. First of all she tried the porridge in Father Bear's great big bowl. "Ow!" she cried. "It's far too hot."

Next she tried the porridge in Mother Bear's medium-sized bowl. But that was far too lumpy. Last of all she picked up the tiny little spoon and tried some of Baby Bear's porridge. It was just right, so she ate it all up.

Then Goldilocks decided that she needed a rest. She tried to sit in great big Father Bear's chair, but that was far too high. Next she sat in Mother Bear's medium-sized chair but that was much too hard and uncomfortable.

Finally she tried Baby Bear's tiny little chair and that was just right. But Goldilocks was too heavy for it and the chair started to break. It fell to pieces and she landed on the floor with a bump.

Goldilocks then saw the stairs leading up to the bedroom. She went upstairs and there in front of her, in the bedroom, was the most enormous bed. She scrambled up on to it with great difficulty, but it was far too hard.

Next she climbed on to the medium-sized bed, but that was far too soft. Lastly she tried Baby Bear's tiny little bed and that was just right. It was so comfortable that Goldilocks quickly fell fast asleep.

Shortly afterwards the three bears returned from their walk in the woods. Great big Father Bear saw that the breakfast table was untidy. He went over to the table. "Who's been eating my porridge?" he growled.

Mother Bear then looked at her bowl. "And who's been eating my porridge?" she said.

Baby Bear looked at his tiny porridge bowl and sobbed, "Someone's been eating my porridge, and they've eaten it all up!"

The bears looked round the room and suddenly Father Bear growled in a loud voice, "Who's been sitting in my chair? The cushion is all crumpled."

Mother Bear looked at her medium-sized chair and said, "And who's been sitting in my chair?"

Baby Bear looked at his chair which was lying on the floor in pieces and he sobbed, "Someone's been sitting in my chair and they've broken it."

Father Bear walked upstairs to the bedroom and saw that the cover on his great big bed was all crumpled. "Who's been sleeping in my bed?" he growled.

Then Mother Bear looked at her bed and growled, "And who's been sleeping in my bed? Just look at my pillow!"

"Someone's still sleeping in my bed!" said Baby Bear in a squeaky little voice.

Goldilocks was woken up by the sound of Baby Bear's voice but the first thing she saw when she opened her eyes was great big Father Bear looking very cross. Next to him was not-quite-so-big Mother Bear and Baby Bear, looking very upset.

Goldilocks rubbed her eyes. The sight of the three bears standing together frightened her so much that she leaped out of bed and jumped straight out of the bedroom window. Knocking over a flowerpot, she ran out of the garden and into the woods as fast as she could.

The three bears looked out of the window, but Goldilocks had disappeared. "I don't think we shall see that little girl again," said Father Bear. And, of course they never did.

The Princess and the Pea

Many years ago, in a land far away, there lived a most handsome prince. He lived with his mother and father, the king and queen, in a magnificent castle. When the prince came of age it was decided that he should marry. The prince said to the king and queen, "I will only marry a real princess."

The king and queen decided to organise a royal ball. They sent out many invitations to neighbouring kingdoms inviting hundreds of young ladies to attend.

On the evening of the ball maidens of every shape and size arrived. Some were tall and thin, others short and fat; some had fair hair, others were dark; some had blue eyes and others brown. But at the end of the evening the maidens all returned home because the prince had been unable to find one real princess.

The prince decided that he must go in search of a real princess on his own. He set off on his horse, waving to the king and queen as he left the royal palace. "Good luck," cried the king.

For several years the prince travelled. He visited many countries, calling at every castle and palace that he passed in his search for a real princess. He saw many beautiful ladies in this time but none was a true princess. Eventually he gave up his search and, tired and unhappy, returned home to the palace. He said to the king and queen, "I have given up all hope of finding a real princess to be my wife."

Then, one wet night, when the rain was beating against the windows and the wind was howling, a slender figure struggled through the rain and the wind and knocked at the palace gates. The king went to see who was knocking on such a stormy night. Standing there in the light from a flaming torch was a beautiful young girl, drenched through and shivering in the cold air.

"I lost my way in the storm," said the girl.

The king led her into the hall and the queen came to help the girl. "You must have a hot bath and some food and stay the night," she said.

Refreshed and wearing some borrowed clothes, the young girl came down to the dining-hall. She was very beautiful and the young prince fell in love with her straight away. She curtsied in front of the king and queen and said, "I am a princess."

So many other girls had claimed to be princesses that the queen was very suspicious. While the young girl was eating she rushed off to organise a comfortable bed. She asked the servants to pile twenty mattresses one on top of the other on the bed, and then she asked for more feather mattresses to be laid on top. The queen then carefully placed a pea under the bottom mattress.

The pile of mattresses was so tall that the young girl needed a ladder to climb on to it. "I do hope that you have a very comfortable night, my dear," the queen said, as she tucked the young girl into bed. "Goodnight, sleep well." But to herself the queen said, "We'll know in the morning whether she's a real princess or not."

Next morning the young girl came down to breakfast looking very tired. "What is the matter? Did you not sleep very well?" asked the queen.

"No, I didn't," replied the young girl. "There was a hard lump in the mattress and I'm black and blue all over with bruises."

The queen was secretly delighted. The young girl must indeed be a real princess if she could feel a pea through so many mattresses. Only a real princess would have such a delicate skin.

The prince was overjoyed at the news and said to the young girl, "You must be my bride. Please say you will marry me."

The young princess was very happy, and agreed straight away.

They were married in a magnificent ceremony in the palace chapel. The pea was placed on show in a specially made glass cabinet for all the people to come and see, so that they would know their prince had married a real princess.

And the prince and princess lived happily ever after.

The Little Red Hen

Once upon a time there was a little red hen and she lived on a farm. One day she was scratching around in the farmyard, looking for food, when she saw some grains of wheat in the dust. She called all her friends in the farmyard together.

"Just look what I've found," she said. "Who will help me to plant these grains of wheat in the field?" The cat and the rat and the pig looked at each other.

"Not I," said the cat.
"Not I," said the rat.
"Not I," said the pig.

"Very well," said the little red hen, "I shall plant them myself."

And what do you think she did? The little red hen went off to the field to find a good patch of soil in the sun. She planted the grains of wheat with her beak in a long hollow. Then she covered over the seeds carefully, scratching the soil round them.

The little red hen watched the wheat plants growing in the field. Every day she splashed water over them and pecked off any weeds. The wheat grew taller and stronger.

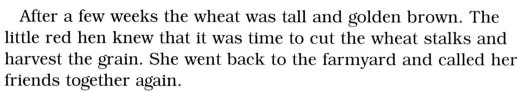

After a few weeks the wheat was tall and golden brown. The little red hen knew that it was time to cut the wheat stalks and harvest the grain. She went back to the farmyard and called her friends together again.

"Who will help me to cut the wheat now that it is ripe?" said the little red hen. The cat and the rat and the pig looked at each other.

"Not I," said the cat.

"Not I," said the rat.

"Not I," said the pig.

"Very well," said the little red hen, "I shall cut the wheat myself."

And what do you think she did? The little red hen went back to the field and snipped through the wheat stems with her beak. She collected them all together, ready to take them to the miller.

Once again she called her friends in the farmyard together. "Who will help me to carry the wheat stalks to the mill for the miller to grind the grains into flour?" she asked. The cat and the rat and the pig just looked at each other.

"Not I," said the cat.

"Not I," said the rat.

"Not I," said the pig.

"Very well," said the little red hen, "I shall carry them myself."

She went back to the field and picked up the big bundle of wheat and carried it all the way to the mill. There the miller ground the grains into flour and poured all the flour into a big sack.

The little red hen then carried the sack of flour to the farmyard. Again she called to her friends in the farmyard. "Who will help me to carry the big sack of flour to the baker for him to make some bread?" she asked. The cat and the rat and the pig just looked at each other.

"Not I," said the cat.

"Not I," said the rat.

"Not I," said the pig.

"Very well," said the little red hen, "I shall carry the flour to the baker myself."

She picked up the big sack of flour and carried it all the way to the bakehouse. The baker made a beautiful, big brown loaf of bread from the flour.

The little red hen carried the loaf back to the farmyard. "Who will help me to eat the loaf of bread?" she asked. The cat and the rat and the pig looked at each other.

"I will," said the cat.

"I will," said the rat.

"I will," said the pig.

And they rushed over to the loaf of bread. But the little red hen said, "No! You will not eat my beautiful brown loaf. I shall eat it all myself." And she pecked away at the loaf until it was all eaten up.

Snow White

It was wintertime and the snow lay deep on the ground. As the snowflakes fell a queen was sitting by one of the palace windows, sewing. She suddenly let out a cry because the needle had pricked her finger and three drops of bright red blood fell on to her sewing.

She looked at the white of the snow, the blood-red stains and the black of the window frame and thought, "If I have a child I want it to have skin as white as snow, lips as red as blood and hair as black as the window frame."

Sometime afterwards the queen did have a baby daughter and her wishes were fulfilled. The king and queen called their baby Snow White. Sadly, the queen died not long after her baby's birth.

The king remarried a year later. His new queen was very beautiful, and to make sure there was nobody more beautiful than her she would ask the magic mirror hanging on the wall of her room:

"Mirror, mirror, on the wall,
Who is the fairest of them all?"

Every time the mirror replied:

"Thou O queen; thou art the fairest."

This pleased the queen very much because she knew it told the truth.

As Snow White grew up she became more and more beautiful, until one day, when the queen asked the magic mirror who was the fairest in the land, it replied:

"No longer art thou fairest as you stand,
Snow White is the loveliest in the land."

The queen was very angry, and day by day she became more upset as Snow White's beauty increased. So she called for one of her huntsmen.

"Take Snow White into the deepest part of the forest and kill her," she ordered. "I can no longer bear to look at her."

The huntsman took Snow White deep into the forest. But when he pulled out his knife, Snow White began to cry. She begged him not to kill her.

The huntsman was a kindly fellow and put his knife back in its sheath. "Run off into the wood," he said, "and never return." He thought that Snow White would soon be eaten by a wild animal, and would never be seen again. Then he killed a wild boar and cut out its heart and liver to take back to the queen as proof that he had killed Snow White.

Snow White wandered through the forest until she reached the far side. There, to her surprise, she came across a little cottage. She knocked on the door but there was no reply. She opened the door and peeped inside. She was amazed to see a table with seven places neatly laid out, and seven small chairs round it.

Snow White was very tired and hungry so she went into the cottage. She ate a little food from each plate and took a small sip from each glass, and then fell fast asleep on one of the seven small beds at the far side of the room.

After dark the owners of the cottage returned. They were seven dwarfs who went up into the mountain each day to dig for gold and silver. The dwarfs each took a candle from a shelf by the door, and in the flickering light they saw Snow White fast asleep. "What a beautiful child!" they all cried.

"Shh! Don't wake her," said one of them. "Let her sleep until the morning."

In the morning Snow White
woke up to see the faces of the seven dwarfs
round her. She was frightened at first but she soon
realised that the dwarfs meant her no harm. She told them how
her wicked stepmother had made the huntsman take her into the
forest to kill her, but he had let her go free instead. "I went as far
away as I could," Snow White continued, "and eventually I found
your cottage."

The dwarfs wanted to help Snow White after hearing her sad
story. "Will you stay here with us and help keep our house clean
and tidy?" they asked. Snow White was delighted with their
kindness and agreed to help them. Fearing for her safety, the
dwarfs warned Snow White not to open the door to any strangers.

Snow White was very happy. She cleaned the cottage each day,
and every evening when the dwarfs returned from the mountain,
she had cooked a hot meal for them.

The queen believed that Snow White was dead and once more she was the most beautiful lady in the land. After many days had passed, she decided she would ask the magic mirror again:

"Mirror, mirror, on the wall,
Who is the fairest of them all?"

She was very angry when the mirror replied:

"O queen, thou art exceeding fair,
But high up in the mountain air,
Where the sun is very bright,
Still lives the beautiful Snow White."

The queen immediately decided to kill Snow White herself. She disguised herself as an old pedlar woman, putting on old clothes and making her face dirty. She filled an old basket with goods to sell and set off for the mountains. Outside the dwarfs' cottage she called out, "Lots of pretty things to buy." Snow White looked out of the window and saw an old lady holding up some pretty ribbons.

"This poor old woman can't do me any harm," she said to herself. She opened the door and the old woman persuaded her to buy some pretty laces for her dress.

"Let me put them on for you," said the wicked queen. But she pulled the laces so tight that Snow White couldn't breathe and fell to the floor.

That evening the dwarfs returned to find Snow White lying on the floor as if she were dead. They immediately cut the tight laces and Snow White started to breathe again. She told them about the pedlar woman and they said, "That must be the queen. You must be careful, Snow White, she is determined to kill you."

The next morning the queen stood in front of the mirror.
"Mirror, mirror, on the wall,
Who is the fairest of them all?"
she recited, thinking that it would be herself. But when the mirror said that Snow White was still the most beautiful, the queen flew into a dreadful rage.

This time she disguised herself as an old woman selling combs, and went back to the dwarfs' cottage. She knocked on the door and once again Snow White saw an old lady and let her in.

"Let me comb your pretty hair," said the queen. But she had poisoned the combs and when she combed Snow White's hair she dug the comb in. Snow White fell to the floor and did not move.

In the evening the dwarfs found her lying on the floor of the cottage and they were very worried. They saw the comb and when they took it out Snow White quickly came round.

The dwarfs realised that the queen must have visited the cottage again and they were cross with Snow White. "Do not let anyone into the cottage," they said as they left her the following morning. "You must be very careful."

When the queen returned home she looked into the mirror.
"Mirror, mirror, on the wall,
Who is the fairest of them all?"
she asked. But when the mirror replied:
"Thou art exceeding fair, O queen,
But Snow White is the fairest to be seen",
the queen screamed in anger. Three times she had tried to kill Snow White and each time she had failed. This time she would succeed.

Disguising herself as a farmer's wife, she set off once again for the dwarfs' cottage. At the window of the cottage she showed Snow White the lovely ripe apples she had in her basket. "You must try one of these juicy apples," she cried.

"But I am not allowed to open the door or to buy anything," Snow White replied.

"Why ever not, my dear?" asked the wicked queen. "Look, I will share this one with you." She took from her basket a poisoned apple and cut it in half, and passed the poisoned half through the window to Snow White.

Snow White could not resist the juicy red apple and she took a bite of it. Immediately she fell to the floor, deathly pale, and did not move.

The queen returned to the palace and stood in front of her magic mirror.

"Mirror, mirror, on the wall,
Who is the fairest of them all?"

she asked. This time the mirror answered:

"Thou, O queen, art indeed the fairest."

The queen was happy at last.

When the dwarfs returned from their day's work they found Snow White on the floor, but they could not find out what had happened to her. They did all they could but Snow White did not recover.

After three days the dwarfs decided to make a glass coffin for Snow White, so they would still be able to see her beauty. They carried her up the mountain and laid the coffin on some rocks. In turn, they each watched over her as she lay there, her snow-white skin, her blood-red lips and her black hair still as beautiful as when they had first seen her.

One day a prince rode by. He could not believe how beautiful Snow White was and he fell instantly in love with her. He pleaded with the dwarfs to let him take Snow White with him, promising that he would look after her for the rest of his life. But the dwarfs said, "All the gold in the world would not make us part with Snow White."

The prince kept asking and the dwarfs saw that he was truly upset by their refusal to allow Snow White to be taken away. They took pity on him and agreed that the prince could look after their beloved Snow White. This made the prince very happy.

As the coffin was being moved down the mountainside by the dwarfs and the prince's servants, one of them stumbled and jolted the coffin. A piece of the poisoned apple which had become stuck in Snow White's throat was loosened and caused her to cough. She awoke with a start, wondering where she was.

The prince and the seven dwarfs were delighted and told her the whole story; then the prince asked Snow White to marry him. She agreed at once.

A huge wedding reception was arranged at the king's palace and Snow White's stepmother was invited to attend. Before she left the palace in her fine clothes, the wicked queen looked into the magic mirror and asked:

"Mirror, mirror, on the wall,
Who is the fairest of them all?"

The reply came:

"O queen, though thou art beautiful,
The bride who will be there
Is even more exceeding fair."

At this, the queen was so angry that at first she decided not to go to the wedding, but she was curious to see the new princess. When she arrived, the queen recognised Snow White at once, and was astonished to see that she was still alive. Snow White immediately recognised her stepmother, and the prince ordered the palace guards to seize the queen and drive her from the kingdom.

The wicked queen was never seen again, and the prince and Snow White, his new princess, lived happily ever after. She was, without doubt, the most beautiful lady in the kingdom.

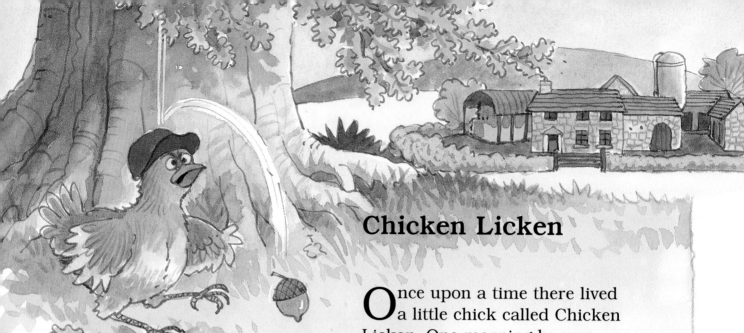

Chicken Licken

Once upon a time there lived a little chick called Chicken Licken. One morning he was playing under an oak-tree when an acorn fell from a branch and hit him on the head.

"Help," he thought. "The sky must be falling down." So off he rushed to tell the king.

On the way there Chicken Licken met Henny Penny. "Hello, Chicken Licken. Where are you off to in such a hurry?" asked Henny Penny.

"Oh dear, Henny Penny, the sky is falling down and I'm off to tell the king," said Chicken Licken.

"Well, in that case I am going to come with you," said Henny Penny. So off they went to find the king's palace.

As they hurried along they met Cocky Locky. "Where are you two going?" he asked.

"The sky is falling down and we're off to tell the king," said Chicken Licken.

"That sounds exciting," said Cocky Locky. "I shall come with you." So Chicken Licken, Henny Penny and Cocky Locky hurried on their way to tell the king that the sky was falling down.

They had not travelled very far when they met Ducky Lucky. "Hello, Chicken Licken. Where are you three going in such a hurry?" said Ducky Lucky.

"Oh dear, Ducky Lucky, the sky is falling down and we're off to tell the king," said Chicken Licken.

80

"Then I shall come with you," said Ducky Lucky. So Chicken Licken, Henny Penny, Cocky Locky and Ducky Lucky hurried on together to find the king, to tell him that the sky was falling down.

No sooner had they reached the edge of a pond than they met Drakey Lakey. "Hello, Chicken Licken," said Drakey Lakey. "Where are you all hurrying?"

Chicken Licken replied, "Oh dear, Drakey Lakey, we're off to tell the king that the sky is falling down."

"Then I shall come with you," said Drakey Lakey. So Chicken Licken, Henny Penny, Cocky Locky, Ducky Lucky and Drakey Lakey hurried on together to find the king, to tell him that the sky was falling down.

They were just passing by a farmyard when they met Goosey Loosey. "Hello, Chicken Licken," said Goosey Loosey. "Where are you all hurrying?"

Chicken Licken replied, "Oh dear, Goosey Loosey, we're off to tell the king that the sky is falling down."

"Then I shall come with you," said Goosey Loosey.

So Chicken Licken, Henny Penny, Cocky Locky, Ducky Lucky, Drakey Lakey and Goosey Loosey hurried on together to find the king, to tell him that the sky was falling down.

Running across a field they saw Turkey Lurkey. "Hello, Chicken Licken," said Turkey Lurkey. "Where are you all hurrying?"

Chicken Licken replied, "Oh dear, Turkey Lurkey, we're off to tell the king that the sky is falling down."

"Then I shall come with you," said Turkey Lurkey. So Chicken Licken, Henny Penny, Cocky Locky, Ducky Lucky, Drakey Lakey, Goosey Loosey and Turkey Lurkey hurried on together to find the king, to tell him that the sky was falling down.

They were passing a bushy hedge when out stepped Foxy Loxy. "Hello, Chicken Licken," said Foxy Loxy. "Where are you all hurrying?"

Chicken Licken replied, "Oh dear, Foxy Loxy, we're off to tell the king that the sky is falling down."

Foxy Loxy said, "That's interesting. Follow me, I know where the king can be found." So Chicken Licken, Henny Penny, Cocky Locky, Ducky Lucky, Drakey Lakey, Goosey Loosey and Turkey Lurkey all followed Foxy Loxy in a line.

But Foxy Loxy didn't take them to find the king. Instead he led them straight to his den in the woods. His wife and their little foxes were waiting there, and the fox family ate Chicken Licken, Henny Penny, Cocky Locky, Ducky Lucky, Drakey Lakey, Goosey Loosey and Turkey Lurkey for their supper.

Poor Chicken Licken. He never did find the king to tell him that the sky was falling down.

Cinderella

There was once a pretty young girl called Cinderella. Her mother had died and her father had remarried. Her stepmother had two plain-looking daughters from her first marriage, and all three were very unkind to Cinderella.

The two stepsisters spent their time enjoying themselves while Cinderella had to do all the housework. They bought lots of new clothes while poor Cinderella had to wear old, threadbare clothes which were full of holes. Her real name was Ella, but she became known to all as Cinderella because, after her work was done, she would sit dreaming by the warmth of the fire, among the cinders and ashes.

One day the stepsisters received an invitation to a royal ball which was to be held in honour of the prince, who was looking for a wife. The stepsisters were very excited. Perhaps one of them would be chosen to be the prince's bride.

On the evening of the ball Cinderella was told to help her stepsisters get ready, and had to run round after them, fetching their shoes, gloves, handbags and coats, and their jewellery.

After the sisters had been collected in a royal carriage, Cinderella went into the kitchen and sat down in the cinders and cried. As she was sobbing, Cinderella heard a voice asking, "Why are you crying, Cinderella?"

"I so wanted to go to the ball," replied Cinderella.

"And you shall go to the ball," said the woman.

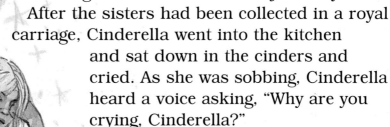

Cinderella looked up and was amazed to see a beautiful woman standing by her.

"I am your fairy godmother," she said. "Now, if you want to go to the ball we must act quickly. Go into the garden and fetch a large pumpkin."

Cinderella ran outside and came back with the largest pumpkin she could carry. The fairy godmother touched it with her magic wand and it changed into a golden coach. "Now we need a rat," she said, and her wand changed that into a coachman.

"Now find me six white mice," said the fairy godmother. These she changed one by one into six magnificent white horses, which the coachman harnessed to the coach. "And now six lizards," she continued. At the touch of her wand they changed into footmen.

Cinderella was amazed. She couldn't believe what was happening. "But how can I go to the ball dressed like this?" she said. And a touch of the magic wand transformed her into a beautiful young woman wearing a shimmering ball-gown, with jewels in her hair. Finally, her fairy godmother gave her a pair of dainty glass slippers.

As she helped Cinderella into the coach, the fairy godmother said, "You must be home by midnight because the magic will end at the first stroke of twelve o'clock. Remember that."

So Cinderella travelled to the ball in style. Everyone was intrigued by the beautiful stranger in her shimmering dress. "Who can she be?" said her stepsisters. They were jealous because Cinderella danced with the prince all evening. He had eyes for nobody else. He had never seen such beauty and fell in love with Cinderella straight away.

Cinderella was carried away by the excitement of the evening. She had fallen in love with the prince and had forgotten everything else. Suddenly she was aware that the palace clock stood at two minutes to midnight. Panicking, she rushed out of the palace ballroom, and as she ran down the steps she heard the clock striking twelve. Her clothes began to change back to rags, the coach changed into a pumpkin and the horses, coachman and footmen changed back into white mice, a rat and lizards. One of her glass slippers fell off but she was in such a panic that she barely noticed.

The prince shouted after her, "Come back! Come back!" but Cinderella kept on running.

When she reached her home she crept to her place by the fire, and there she found that although she was back in her rags, she still wore one glass slipper.

The prince was intent on finding the beautiful girl with whom he had fallen in love "I will marry the girl whose foot fits the slipper," he announced. The glass slipper had been found on the palace steps and that was the only clue he had. So he set off round the country in search of the mysterious owner of the dainty glass slipper. Every young woman in the kingdom tried on the slipper, but it was either too big or too small.

At last the royal party arrived at the house where Cinderella lived. Each of the stepsisters tried on the slipper but it didn't fit.

"Have you any sisters?" the prince asked.

"We have one," said the sisters, "but she is far too busy working."

"I insist that she tries it on," said the prince. "Everyone, without exception, must try on the slipper."

The prince slid the slipper on to Cinderella's foot and it fitted perfectly. Everyone was astonished when Cinderella put the other glass slipper on her other foot. Then the prince looked up at Cinderella's face and recognised the beautiful girl that he had danced with at the ball. He knelt, and holding her hands he asked Cinderella to marry him.

Suddenly her fairy godmother appeared. One touch of her magic wand changed Cinderella's ragged clothes into a beautiful dress. "There you are," she said. "Now you're fit to be a princess."

Cinderella was delighted to accept the prince's proposal of marriage. She climbed on to his horse and he led her to the palace.

Their wedding was magnificent. Even the stepsisters agreed that Cinderella looked beautiful, and they begged her to forgive them. And of course, the prince and his new princess lived happily ever after.

The Ugly Duckling

Hidden in among the stems and leaves on the banks of the river, a duck was sitting on the eggs in her nest. She was keeping them warm so that they would hatch. When at last the eggs began to crack she was very pleased. One after another the little ducklings pushed their heads out through the eggshells. All except one, the biggest egg, which didn't hatch with the others.

The mother duck was puzzled by the large egg, but she sat on it until it hatched as well. Out popped the last duckling. "What a large, ugly, grey duckling," she thought. But she was excited, because now she could take her new family down to the river.

It was warm and sunny as she waddled down to the water's edge next morning. She was followed by the ducklings who were rushing along to keep up. And soon all of them were swimming along behind the mother duck, even the ugly one.

A passing duck remarked, "What pretty ducklings! But isn't that grey one ugly?"

The mother duck was upset by this and thought, "Perhaps it will become beautiful as it grows older."

She took her brood back to the farmyard. As they waddled through the farmyard gate all the other animals chuckled as the ugly duckling passed by. "What an ugly duckling!" they chorused together. Some of the birds, including the big red cockerel, pecked at him every time he came close.

The ugly duckling grew bigger and bigger and as each day went by he became more and more unhappy. He didn't know what to do. There was nowhere for him to go. Eventually he simply decided to run away. He ran and ran until he was very tired. Finally he was unable to go any further and he crawled into some reeds to hide. He had reached a marshy place close to the river where a large group of wild ducks and geese lived.

When he woke up he found a group of wild ducks looking at him. "You're so ugly," they cackled. And they laughed at him too.

"Oh dear," he thought, "they all think I'm so ugly."

The ugly duckling was very lonely. "It's time to move on again," he thought. He ran away from the marsh, flapping his tiny wings. Over fields, across roads, through hedges, down winding lanes he trudged, day after day. Everywhere he went the birds and other creatures stopped and stared at the ugly duckling. Some scuttled away because they thought he looked so strange.

Tired and very cold, the ugly duckling came to a tiny cottage near the edge of a wood. The door was slightly open so he walked inside. In the dim light from a small oil lamp he could see an old lady, and by her feet were a hen and a big ginger cat.

The old lady was startled to see the ugly duckling but said, "You are welcome to stay as long as you like, but you must lay me an egg every day."

The hen and the cat laughed at the ugly duckling because he looked so odd.

"Are you able to lay eggs?" asked the hen.

"No, I can't," said the ugly duckling.

"And you can't purr either," the ginger cat said.

"You'll have to go," they said together.

So the ugly duckling had to leave. Off into the cold he went. Winter was approaching and most of the leaves had blown off the trees, leaving the branches bare. Overnight the ground became white and hard with frost.

One morning, cold and hungry, his spirits were raised when he saw a flock of huge birds with beautiful, long necks. Their white feathers glistened in the morning sun. As he approached they ran along the surface of the lake and soared into the air, gracefully flapping their wings.

The ugly duckling found life very hard as winter wore on. When the lake froze over, he became so tired that he fell asleep on the ice. A farmer found him in the morning and tucked him inside his jacket to carry him home.

In their kitchen the farmer's wife placed the ugly duckling into a basket lined with straw. He quickly warmed up and drank some milk that she put in a bowl for him.

The farmer's children tried to play games with him but he didn't understand and tried to fly out through a closed window. He fluttered to the floor, then ran out through the open door, into the fields.

Spring came and the weather was much warmer. As the ugly duckling became bigger and stronger his wings were much stronger too. He was now able to fly properly. One day while soaring up into the air, he spotted some beautiful white birds on the water below. They were just like the white birds he had seen before.

Flying down to the lake, he landed with a great splash. As the water settled, instead of seeing an ugly grey duckling reflected in the surface, he saw a beautiful white bird with a long, slender neck. He looked just like the other birds nearby.

A child on the lakeside called out, "Look, Mummy, a beautiful new swan has arrived." Then the duckling knew that he was a swan, not an ugly duckling after all.

The other swans glided across the water towards him and said, "Come and join us." For the first time he was not being laughed at by others. He was happy.

Little Red Riding Hood

Little Red Riding Hood's granny was feeling poorly. Luckily she lived nearby, in a pretty little cottage on the edge of the wood. The way to Granny's cottage went through the wood, along a narrow path that followed a tiny stream.

Little Red Riding Hood's mother was worried that Granny might not be well enough to make her own tea. "Little Red Riding Hood," she called. "Please would you take some tea over to Granny's house. I've made a cake and some sandwiches for her. They are in the basket on the chair by the door. Make sure you wrap up warm in your new cloak with the pretty red hood which Granny made for you. And don't wander from the path," her mother added.

"Of course I won't," Little Red Riding Hood said. "I would be frightened of getting lost."

Little Red Riding Hood set off into the wood, carrying the basket with her granny's tea. She skipped and danced along. She was always happy when she visited Granny.

She had not walked very far into the wood when out of the bushes jumped a very large wolf. Little Red Riding Hood gave a little shriek and cried out, "Oh, you frightened me! I nearly dropped my basket."

"I am very sorry," said the wolf craftily. "I didn't mean to scare you. Where are you going?"

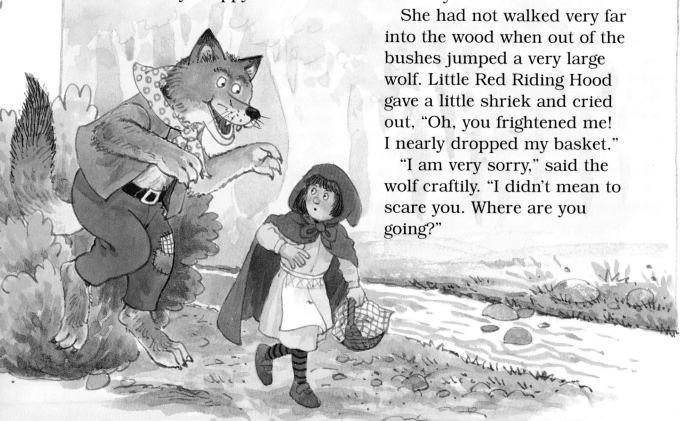

"To my granny's," Little Red Riding Hood replied. The wolf seemed friendly so she was not afraid of him. "My granny is not very well and I am taking her something to eat."

"Where does your granny live, little girl?" asked the wolf.

"In the first cottage you see as you leave the wood," replied Little Red Riding Hood.

"That's quite near here," the wolf exclaimed. "Why don't I go on ahead to let Granny know that you are coming? Be careful walking through the wood," added the wolf, "and make sure that you don't leave the path. We want you to arrive safely at Granny's cottage, don't we?"

Off rushed the wolf through the trees and he soon disappeared from view. The wolf knew that the woodcutter was nearby so he took a shortcut through the trees to Granny's cottage. He took a deep breath and knocked at the door.

The old lady called out, "Who is it?"

The wolf imitated Little Red Riding Hood's voice and replied, "It's only me. I've brought you some nice food for your tea."

Granny's hearing wasn't very good and she called out, "Come in, my dear, the door is not locked." The wolf needed no second invitation and in he went. He was very hungry because he hadn't eaten for several days and he immediately swallowed Granny in one huge gulp.

Not long afterwards there was another knock on the front door of Granny's cottage. It was Little Red Riding Hood.

"Who's there?" called the wolf, trying his best to sound like a little old lady.

"It's Little Red Riding Hood, Granny."

"Come in, my dear," said the wolf, "the door is not locked."

Little Red Riding Hood stopped for a moment. There was something strange about Granny's voice. "Perhaps it's because she's not well," she thought. She turned the door-handle and in she went.

The wolf was in bed with Granny's nightcap on his head, her glasses on the end of his nose, and he was wearing her lacy pink nightgown. He had drawn the curtains across the window to make it as dark as possible and the bedclothes were pulled right up over his body.

"Put the basket down and come over here to be close to me, Little Red Riding Hood," said the wolf. Little Red Riding Hood started to do as she was asked, but then she hesitated.

"Oh, Granny, what big, hairy arms you have!" she said.

"All the better to hold you with!" replied the wolf.

"Oh, Granny, what huge ears you have!"

"All the better to hear you with!" replied the wolf.

"Oh, Granny, what large eyes you have!"

"All the better to see you with!" replied the wolf.

"Oh, Granny, what big teeth you have!"

"All the better to eat you with!" replied the wolf.

The wolf was still hungry and with great speed he quickly threw off the bedclothes and jumped out of bed. He caught Little Red Riding Hood by surprise and swallowed her whole. Now he was full up the wolf decided to take a nap, so he climbed back on to the bed and fell fast asleep.

But as the wolf lay on the bed dreaming and snoring loudly the woodcutter passed by. "I wonder what's wrong with Granny," he thought. "She doesn't usually snore like that." He went into the cottage quietly and when he saw the wolf lying on the bed and no sign of Granny he realised what had happened.

"At last I've caught you," the woodcutter cried. And before the wolf knew what was happening the woodcutter brought his axe down on the wolf's head. Then he slit the wolf open and carefully pulled out Little Red Riding Hood and Granny. Neither had come to any harm.

Granny saw the sandwiches and the cake that Little Red Riding Hood had brought for her. "What we need now is a big pot of tea," she said, and went to put the kettle on the hob. She made Little Red Riding Hood promise that she would never again be deceived by a wolf.

"Now hurry back to your mother," Granny said after tea. "The woodcutter will take you safely home."

And what a strange tale Little Red Riding Hood would have to tell her mother!